David Noone grew up in a sm. Kildare, Ireland. At 14 he was first admitted for what would become a continuous series of psychiatric hospital admissions to receive treatment for Recurrent Depressive Disorder.

Having little access to formal education within the confines of the hospital, Noone immersed himself in the works of Poe, Camus, Baudelaire, and Rimbaud whilst listening to the music of *The Virgin Prunes*, *Throbbing Gristle*, and *The Birthday Party*.

At 18 he moved to Dublin and worked around the arts world until the end of his twenties as front of house in the Focus Theatre serving drinks at various art galleries throughout the city. Over this period he had several poems published in literary journals and acted as lead singer and songwriter for his bands *Poppy* and *David Noone and The Night Porters* as well as touring Britain and Ireland with his show *David Noone sings Nick Cave*.

Though mostly retired from performance he still takes to the stage from time to time. He continues to live and write in Dublin.

# SAINT OF THE CITY

Copyright © 2017 David Noone

All rights reserved

ISBN: 978-0-244-31325-8

*Saint Of The City* is presented as a work of fiction and any likeness to any person living or dead is entirely coincidental.

10 9 8 7 6 5 4 3 2 1

First Printing

Cover and Interior Art © 2017 Steve Hussy

No part of this book may be used or reproduced in any manner whatsoever without written permission from the publisher, except in the case of quotations embodied in critical articles and reviews.

For all queries contact:

Murder Slim Press,

22 Bridge Meadow, Hemsby, Norfolk. NR29 4NE

United Kingdom

Edited by:

Steve Hussy

Published by Murder Slim Press 2017

www.murderslim.com

**Printed in the UK by the MPG Books Group, King's Lynn.**

# Darkness at Noone
– An Introduction by Cathi Unsworth –

I like to think of life as an ongoing novel, in which every twist is a revelation gleaned from a previous experience. Case in point, I have still to meet the author, blues troubadour and black-hearted wit David Noone in person. Yet, having just taken his debut novella, *Saint of the City* down in one narcotic gulp, I feel that we might first have been introduced long ago, by a couple of his fellow Irishmen who share an innate grasp of stylishness, satire and subversion.

In 1995, I had the good fortune to spend a while talking to the wonderful Gavin Friday about his third solo album, *Shag Tobacco*; a spellbinding depiction of a decadent after-hours Dublin peopled with all kinds of sliders, shape-shifters, cross-dressers and drifters. During the course of his illuminatory spiel on everyone from Enrico Caruso to T-Rex, Gavin extolled the genius of Patrick McCabe's *The Butcher Boy*, the story of a delinquent child which, he claimed, put that poseur Quentin Tarantino into the shade. Looking back on it now, I realise that Francie Brady, the narrator of that darkly comical and fiercely original tale, was probably about the same age as David Noone would have been back then.

When David asked me to read *Saint of the City* he merely opined that I might find the lead character, Sean Aloysius Ignatius Augustus Connolly "dislikable". Sean's employer, bookshop owner and world-weary sage Frank, tells it to him this way: *"Go home* and hit the scratcher, you look like the worst form of scuttery shite I've seen since I had to plunge the jacks after the wife got over that last bout of constipation."

Which is why I immediately loved this book.

David's command of language, and his perfectly gothic vision of a charming psycho carving his way through a contemporary Dublin swathed in the blue smoke of a million cigarettes, chimed perfectly with the meomory of both Gavin Friday's haunted dancehalls and the bright eyes of Pat McCabe's pig-slaughtering youth. Could this be the impossible lovespawn of Mr Pussy and Da Brady run amok? It is certainly noir fiction with both poise and purpose, not something you can really have too much of in the contemporary canon. A scaborous little tale, swift and compulsive in the telling, which manages to pack a lot of points into a svelte amount of pages.

For one, it lifts up a mirror to our narcissitic times. It skillfully contrasts the concerns of today's self-harming youth, pouring out tales of mutual misery in safe spaces overseen by politically correct mentors, to previous generations who turned all that hormonal rage and loathing into blistering musical ephipenies instead, as by turn, Sean attends twelve-step meetings and blasts out Teenage Jesus and James Chance from the turntable in Frank's shop.

"If they can't handle a bit of The Contortions, they can't handle a good book," he reasons, inarguably.

As well as knowing his No Wave, Noone also thoughtfully provides a primer on outsider literature and its place in adolescent experience via Sean's many sexual conquests, who get as good a going over on the bookshelf as they do in the bedroom.

"Aren't you a little old for Sylvia Plath?" he asks one.

"She knew what she was doing," comes the reply.

"What, topping herself?"

"Obviously."

Later, she hands him a copy of The Marquis de Sade's *Justine* as he is leaving, with orders to read if before she sees him again. When he replies that he already has, she retorts: *"Well you had better look at it again... It seems you've forgotten most of it."*

David's lightly worn but obviously deeply imbibed knowledge of the darkest strands of music and literature and the importance of both come as something of a relief to an older author still reeling from the fact that, during the 2011 riots that tore through London, probably the safest place to stand to avoid any trouble was in the middle of Waterstones. It's good to know that these things still matter, and that, swaggering and artful as David's writing is, this is no Tarantino-type of empty nihilism, but a search for truth and beauty among every kind of transgression. Which is also, crucially, as funny as fuck.

Recalling their first meeting on the sleevenotes for Gavin Friday's 2011 *Catholic* LP, Pat McCabe remembers that: "Gavin's hands were nearly as big as his hair." Now, as I say, I've yet to meet Mr Noone in the flesh. But those You Tube clips I've watched of him singing suggest similar attributes.

In my experience, there is no such thing as coincidence.

### *Cathi Unsworth, London, January 2017*

Dedicated to the late Prof Anthony Clare, Dr Melissa Darmody, all at St. Edmundsbury & St John Of God psychiatric hospitals, Marlboro Red, Camel Yellow, Lucky Strike Red, Golden Virginia & the plethora of sleeping pills, sedatives, anti-depressants & mood stabilisers I've been on for the last 18 years.

Without them I would not have survived to write this book.

"I wanna tell you about a girl."

Nick Cave

*From Her To Eternity*

## •••••Chapter One

Danielle, a long legged redhead, lay beneath my none-too-clean sheets. 26. Thin hips. Smooth skin. Neatly trimmed bush. A degree in English and History, a masters in something ridiculous and two brain cells that'd long since stopped communicating. This was not an uncommon occurrence, particularly for teachers. Give them a year outside the university gates, a job crisis and suddenly they've forgotten what a bookshop looks like. I'd seen it a thousand times and wondered how I could have spent six years drinking two bottles of wine a day and still manage to have ten times the brains they had. Danielle was just another idiot with a few letters after her name. It was sad but that was all she was.

Of course not everyone is like this, I had just given up looking for those that were different.

But that bush. Fuck. That bush was a sight to behold. Nothing more beautiful to look at than a redhead with a bush. Obviously I'm in the minority with this sort of thinking but I've always been a living anachronism and I'm too old to change now.

We both knew we'd never see each other again and I was feeling impatient. I'd let her rest for the minute though.

It was the least I could do considering the view she was giving me.

•••

I got my smokes.

Now I had to figure out what to do with the day.

I ran my fingers through my hair, trying to untangle a stubborn curl, and beneath an apathetic sun I began the walk from Ranelagh to Grafton Street. There was nothing else to do.

I decided I'd drop into the second-hand bookshop where I did a bit of part time work for spending money. Under the table, obviously. The shop was one of those "blink and you'll miss it" places off Georges Street. As soon as I entered I was greeted by Frank's Northside growl.

"Well if it isn't Mr. Sean Aloysius Ignatius Augustus Connolly! How's the world been treating you?"

My voice immediately modulated to his;

"Not so bad, same as usual. Yourself?"

"Same as, my boy. Same as. Can't complain and who'd listen to me if I did."

I smiled.

"Know the way buddy."

"Any women on the scene lately?"

"You know me, Frank, I'm practically a priest these days."

"A nun you mean? You're full of shite anyway you little bollocks," Frank said. "I've seen you about, you'd charm the knickers off anyone who wore a pair, though doubt you go for that sort you dirty cunt."

"Nah, not my type."

"The ones with the knickers or the ones without?"

I looked at him with a crooked smile and gave him the answer he wanted.

"They all end up the same in the end, buddy."

Frank laughed and said: "Fair point."

We went on talking shite for another fifteen minutes before I asked him what times he wanted me in next week. Frank with his red Luke Kelly beard and me with the vertical mass of curls that invariablely made me look like I'd stumbled out of the Eraserhead cast party.

"Could do with you locking up Thursday evening, got a bit of business to do, you know yourself."

"Yeah, that's no hassle Frank."

"One more thing, my boy."

"Yeah Frank?"

"Go home and hit the scratcher, you look like the worst form of scuttery shite I've seen since I had to plunge the jacks after the wife got over that last bout of constipation of hers."

"Thanks Frank."

"I mean it brother. Don't want to see you again 'til Thursday and no skirt chasing in the meanwhile, right?"

"No need to do any chasing. Since your wife had that shite she's been knocking over for her biweekly shag again."

"You're some bollocks Sean lad," came the growl.

"Fuck, you can have her anyway, I could do with the break."

After another half hour or so more slagging, I left Frank and started home. When I got in Danielle was still there. She'd just gotten out of the shower, her hair still wet. She asked what I was up to for the rest of the day.

"Meeting Kate later on, haven't seen her in ages."

"Who?"

"Girl I know from way back when. Been meaning to catch up with her."

"Ah ok, thought she might be another one of your girlfriends."

I lit a cigarette. Looked at her. Looked straight through her. What did she care whether I was meeting another girlfriend or not? She continued nonetheless.

"I know your type."

She didn't.

"Really?"

I was beyond incredulous now.

"Fancy a pint sometime later in the week?"

"Why not?"

We exchanged numbers and I told her I'd be in touch. It was a lie. But she knew it.

"Cool. I look forward to it."

•••

"Coffee, Sean?"

Kate was in her late 30's but could have passed for 20. Blonde, intelligent with a set of legs like a lothario's Camino. She was wearing a wool dress that stopped just before the knee with no tights or shoes. I wondered what else she'd neglected to put on.

"Yeah, love one."

She had a nice little one bed place. Bedroom and living area where she kept her books piled in semi neat stacks beside the couch. I began rolling a cigarette as Kate walked into over to her little kichenette to make our coffees.

She came over and gave me my mug, sat down with hers and I lit my smoke.

"So, one night stand or are you actually going out with someone?"

"What are you talking about?"

Kate was smiling at me. That knowing smile of hers. What Daniel didn't know Kate did.

"You need to shower more often, Sean."

*Saint of the City*

We both laughed and Kate sparked up a cigarette. We began talking about the old days back when we used to play in a noise band together. The usual sort of bullshit people talk when they haven't seen each other in a while with me looking at her legs throughout. She knew it too. And that was the fun. Nothing else needed to happen. Kate was probably the only person I actually liked. Frank was alright but only in small doses. It was different with Kate. We could talk for hours and rarely get bored. Even when that did happen it'd be forgotten about the next time we'd meet.

We kept on talking, I kept on looking and we both kept on smoking. Not a bad way to spend an afternoon really. Legs. Coffee. Cigarettes.

## ●●●●● Chapter Two

Grace, my psychotherapist, suggested that it might be an idea for me to try out one of those community based suicide support groups to see if it would help elongate my periods away from the madhouse. In fairness I hadn't being doing too bad recently. It'd been six months since my last admission but she said it couldn't hurt. So I acquiesced and said I'd go.

I remember knocking on the door and a man, who could have been anywhere between his mid-forties to late-fifties, answered the door.

"Yes?"

"I'm Sean Connolly, I'm here for the group?"

"Oh, of course, come in."

He was as nondescript as you could get. Probably groomed himself that way. Couldn't be intimidating any of the sad little fucks inside. Despair obviously doesn't like a man with presence. He led me to a room with a handful of chairs roughly arranged in a circle. Two blondes and a brunette were there along with another three men. If you could call them men. I couldn't help but take an instant dislike to them. It's a common enough thing with me but these non-beings inspired something that was just about one step short of hatred. Fuck it, I might as well say I hated them and I'm just glad I don't have to sit in a room with them anymore.

I took a seat leaving an empty chair to each side of me and the non-descript man sat down. He turned and spoke to one of the brunettes.

"So..."

He paused looking at her blithely.

"How are you this week, Justine?"

"It's been hard this week Paul, I just keep thinking about it."

"Really, well, if you want to talk about it, I know everyone here has been through a lot and most have felt the same as you are at the moment."

I looked around the room at these pathetic souls and thought what an overarching statement this was. What a fucking ridiculously assumptive one too.

"If you do the group is here to support you and to try and get you through it."

I wouldn't.

"I know, Paul."

Her voice was filled with naïve self-pity and belief. Did she really believe this guy?

"And the group really has been a lifeline to me."

"Is it still everyday, Justine?"

"Most days...."

"Well, that's something Justine."

This cunt was the second best liar I had ever met though he hadn't a patch on me. His condescension made me want to cut off his balls and shove them down his throat just so I could watch him suffocate on his bollocks.

"You must be getting somewhere."

"I don't know where I want to get though, Paul, I really don't."

"One step at a time, Justine," he smiled. "Baby steps all the way. We shouldn't try for anything more than that."

It didn't seem to be going down well with Justine either. She was looking at the floor as she answered.

"I know."

I noticed how this Paul twat seemed to have to, almost like a tic, use peoples first name in every sentence he spoke. To make things more personal probably, more family like.

Next came Stephen. A dipso whose wife had left him. He went on about this and all the pain and misery in his life, with Paul's guidance and affirmations, for about fifteen fucking minutes.

"I tell you no one else would stay off the gargle after what I've been through. But by God I do. You'd think after I ran into that car the kids'd come to see me in the hospital, I raised them for Jesus sake, just because I'd a few whiskeys on me they think that's enough to disown me? No gratitude! And that woman she won't even answer the phone. But I'm strong I tell you. They won't beat me. None of them! Shower of bastards!"

If I wasn't suicidal when I arrived, I certainly was now. How could someone have any sort of faith in humankind after listening to these fuckers?

I know if I was this fuck's wife it would be nothing to do with the idiot's alcohol consumption as to why I'd leave, the boredom would be enough. And what was this guy like in bed? I can't even imagine how bad it must have been for the poor woman. Anyone that arrogant is covering something up, most likely that he has a cock the size of safety pin. She's probably been in more of these groups than he has. And with just cause.

The other brunette wasn't much better, Sarah, "too much weed" according to her.

"Every morning I'd need to skin up. Never knew it could be so addictive. Just one joint after the other - twenty four hours a day – I felt like I was in a black hole."

Then a chick with cropped black hair, somewhere in her late 20's, expensively dressed and looking like she'd just had a make over to attend the group. Her entire get up looked like it cost more than my rent. She wasn't hard on the eyes so I ended up trying my best to just zone out and imagine the bitch's hips moving in crazed ecstatic undulations on top of my cock. She reminded me of someone though.

Paul introduced her as Julianne and with what had become his obvious his mind numbing monotony he asked her how she was.

She looked at the floor and began to speak.

"I just wake up and it's there, it's there every morning, you know like it's always there and I just want to get it over with. Everything's always so hard..."

Yeah. Like I was when I first saw you, bitch, before you started to speak.

"...it's just really difficult you know? The cutting isn't working anymore and when I go outside I don't even see faces anymore, I don't see people, just death. I don't know Paul, I don't know what to do anymore..."

Get it over with for fuck sake! Lock your door, take some pills, cut an artery and you're fucking set! Drink a bottle of bleach if you want to. Just shut up!

"I really don't."

And on and on and on she went.

ON.

    AND.

        ON.

            AND.

                ON.

"I can't feel anything other than this horrible numbness and that's all there is. I really don't know how much longer I can hang on."

Paul offered her a few of those platitudes that everyone seems to be filled these days and she continued.

"I know I should try to fight more but it's just so difficult. I promise I will. I mean I'll try and I'll keep coming here I swear."

After this slow death of a speech and a few more platitudes from Paul he announced how there was a new member (me) with us (them) today.

"Sean, would you like to share anything with the group? It's entirely up to you..."

His altruistic vestige became transparent. This was not the kind hearted suggestion he tried to make it sound. It was a demand.

"There's no pressure."

I'd share alright but I wasn't going to share my story so I decided to share another one.

"Yeah, no problem Paul, everyone seems nice here, I think I can say something."

"Only if you want now, Sean."

Oh fuck off Paul. Just drop the charade. I'm beyond this.

"No, it's fine." I paused and looked at him "Well, I suppose it stems from my childhood really..."

The twat was nodding.

"...When I was about eight my father doused me and him in petrol and tried to set us both alight. I can still smell the fumes."

The faces on the people in the room were hilarious.

I went on, deadpan: "Thank God the matches were wet or I wouldn't be here today, he tried it on my mother too and eventually *did* manage to do it to himself. Fuck, Paul, I saw him as his flesh burned, he was running around screaming and I was just paralysed."

Paul tried, not particularly well, to remain unfazed. I stared at him.

"I was a child watching my Dad on fire. I hated the bastard but watching him flail about like that, just all I could do was cry."

I wished I could've taken a picture of the room.

Paul's eyes had widened: "That's obviously a lot to carry round with you for all these years Sean."

It was starting to get difficult to keep a straight face but they were all lapping it up I just couldn't stop there.

"It has been Paul, yeah, it wears me down at times. I dream of it, can't get it out of my head during the day and I tell you Paul, fuck have I tried. Drink, drugs, everything and nothing works. I don't know how I've gotten this far to be honest, I've been pretty close to the edge, well, most of my life really..."

I couldn't look him in the eye now. I would have erupted in laughter if I had.

"Sorry, you don't mind if I leave it at that today? I haven't actually spoken about this before."

The only true word I'd spoken.

"No, of course not Sean, that's fine..." He'd gone pale. It was fucking hilarious. He continued.

"...You only share what you feel comfortable sharing and I can see how hard it was for you to talk about that. It's a lot to say in one day and I admire you for saying it. If you want to say a bit more next week you can as I said we're all here to support each other and to help if we can."

Or to jerk each other off with tea and sympathy.

"Thanks Paul."

The group dispersed and I thanked God. An hour of unmitigated self-indulgence. Fucking disgusting. I don't think I'd ever witnessed anything like it before. And I knew the next one would be the same. That they'd just keep repeating the same stories over and over again. I could just tell.

It wasn't until later that night I realised who Julianne reminded me of. It was Siobhan. I threw back a fistful of Ativan and tried to sleep.

## ●●●●● Chapter Three

    I remember screaming. My eyes burning from the corrosive tears they were producing. Siobhan's lifeless body lying on the couch and the whole room looking like it had been stained by the clotted blood that had pumped from her wrists.

    I held her for an hour before calling the cops.

    I remember that.

    I remember them coming.

    I remember her already cold flesh.

    I remember shaving off every strand of shoulder length black hair from my head and walking round looking like a terminal cancer patient who'd hit the gear for months.

●●●

    In the ten years that had since passed I had been doing everything I could not to think about her while tending to the weeds in my heart.

    I only ever managed to block out so much though. The memories were always there. And now I was going to this group I knew I wouldn't be able to stop them flooding back in their entirety.

    Fuck.

•••

I had been asked to mind the shop on my own for a couple of weeks. Frank had fucked off somewhere on holidays. It was fine with me. He'd would probably throw me an extra 100 euro for looking after the place for such a duration. It would leave me some good pissing away money and with that sort of cash I'd feel like a king for a week.

There was a regular called Elaine who I'd my eye on for a while now. Dressed sort of goth but with a bit more style to her than the kids you'd see hanging around the Central Bank on the mitch from school. But, then again, she looked like she was in her late 20's so if she hadn't acquired any style by now she never would. Her hair cut in a blue black bob framing a face decorated with kohl eye liner and hooker red lipstick. A bit goth? She was the fucking queen of the goths but then again I had always liked goths.

I got talking to her on several occasions, pretty much every time she came in. I managed to convince her to come out for a drink the weekend Frank was due back. Looking at her I knew she wouldn't be a disappointment. She had good taste in books too. Houelbecq, Camus, Kafka...the writers I held closest to my heart.

The Friday Frank came back he threw me 250 Euro. I was set. I could wine and dine Elaine for a week with that. I sent her a text and we arranged a time and a place to meet.

I suggested a club on O'Connell Street called The Udolfo. It only opened once a week. I'd heard good and bad reviews about the place but I wasn't going for that. She said she'd be there. And that was that.

•••

The Udolfo was packed with black clad young and not so young people who posed around the bar drinking snakebite and cheap cider. I got myself a pint and found a table in the corner. I sat waiting for Elaine. I was the only one there not in uniform. No velvet jacket. No eyeliner. My penchant for black and motorcycle boots were all that stopped me sticking out like a paedophile at a school gate.

The music was fucking atrocious. Nine Inch Nails, Type O Negative and a bunch of other shit. I never got how goth music turned into metal considering how violently heterosexual the genre was. And violently male. When I looked at the younger clientele I wondered how many of them had any idea who Diamanda Galas was. Or The Birthday Party. Or Lydia Lunch.

Bauhaus had brought androgyny back to the fore, taking their cue from Bowie and Roxy Music. These kids looked like they were more into Motorhead and Metallica than T-Rex. On top of that it seemed to me that they thought style was one of those things people in the country used for getting over a fence.

Where were all the beautiful people?

Then Elaine walked in.

She went to the bar and had a drink in her hand before I had time to jump up and get her one. She spotted me at the table and walked over.

"Sorry I'm late."

"Not at all," I smiled and took a swig from my pint.

"... woman's prerogative."

"I could say that was sexist if it didn't benefit me."

And we laughed our first laugh of the night.

"How's your day been, Sean?"

"Not bad, bit hung over this morning but the pint's helping."

"You ready to dance?"

"Not really one for dancing," pulling a curl down onto my forehead.

"Try to avoid it at all costs."

"Well you better change that, it's not a night unless you dance!"

She moved closer to me and whispered.

"I've heard a lot of men say that on their first drink."

"Who said this was my first?"

"Your eyes."

She was close now. I could feel her breath as she spoke.

"They betray nothing, my dear Elaine. Nothing. How do you think I survive working in the shop? You think I do it sober?"

"Well I must say you're a very elegant and loquacious piss head if that's true, almost erudite."

"I've learned to bluff."

"You're so full of shit!"

"Of course I am! I work in a book shop Ms..."

"Greene," she said with a false sigh. "Come on...you should know that by now!"

"Oh yeah, I know all of the customers' surnames. Each and every one. You can always tell an O'Dowd from an O'Reilly and an O'Reilly from an O'Connell."

"Everyone in the shop has a prefix to their last name in there?"

"Of course, we get a lot of American tourists who think they're Irish so we got to keep the charade up. Nothing more fun than telling a tourist that Randal P. McMurphy used to own the place. Well, apart from telling them that George's Arcade is Bono's house."

"Does he know that's not actually a real name?"

"Bono? Probably. I don't know about McMurphy but hey, he came into the world that way, so it's not my place to criticise him."

"You do though."

"Obviously."

"Tell me, Sean, how often does this McMurphy come into the shop?"

"Not too often, few times a year."

"Talkative?"

"Very."

"Boisterous."

"You know him then? It's a real cuckoo's nest in there at times."

I burst out laughing. I couldn't keep it in any longer, glad she'd gotten the joke.

"In passing, does his appearance happen to correspond with your dealers?"

"You mean the book dealers? I'd never have any sort of dealings with any of the type I think you might be referring to."

More laughter. This time from the two of us.

"You really are a bullshit artist aren't you Sean?"

"I try, Elaine, I try."

We talked and laughed and drank and laughed for the next few hours. At last orders, we went out into the Dublin night and I looked at Elaine.

"How're you getting home?"

"I'm walking, I'm only about ten minutes away."

"You are in your fuck, what sort of gentleman would I be if I let you walk home alone? I'll get you a cab."

"There's no need honestly Sean, it's no distance."

"Just you be quiet now, I'll pay for it if you need the cash."

She didn't and didn't ask.

When the taxi pulled up to the curb, Elaine got in and looked at me: "You coming?"

I got in. She gave the driver directions. I paid him. She protested. I told her not to. It was the least I could do being a gentleman and all.

We walked up the steps of her place. Went inside and down the hall to her room. The place was pretty as I'd expected. Seventies wallpaper. Double bed in the corner. Wardrobe. A few trinkets here and there. Two sets of bookshelves, one beside the bed and one at the foot of it.

She saw me looking at these.

"You're wondering where the rest of my books are?"

I wasn't.

"There are another more shelves in the sitting room that are a little sturdier... I just keep my favourites here."

"Yeah?"

And the conversation stopped.

We kissed. Falling onto the bed I felt her tits through her clothes. She undid her blue corset. Her body was in better nick than I'd expected. Curves all in proportion. Stomach barely protruding. This shapely body.

I grabbed at her skirt and yanked it down. She had nothing on beneath but her fishnets and suspenders. I could have fucked her in the bathroom, but I wanted a bed to sleep in.

I opened my shirt. She undid the button and zip of my jeans. Began sucking at his cock. I lifted her off. Turned her on her back and fucked her. My jeans around my ankles. My boots still on. Her still in her stockings.

I came and collapsed. Fumbled for my cigarettes. Found them and my light and lit one. Elaine put on some music on her laptop and brought over an ashtray. I gave her a cig.

Soon I was ready again. More quickly than usual. This time on the floor. From behind. I slapped her.

"Sean," she moaned.

I slapped her again. Said: "SIR! Call me Sir bitch! And take it! Even if you don't deserve it you fucking slut!"

Her body softened and I could tell these were the words she wanted to hear.

"Yes... Sir. No I don't deserve it... Sir."

"But you're gonna get it, bitch."

"Yes Sir. Please."

I could sense she was about to come. She'd been moaning the whole time. Moaning "Sir" and "Please". It was getting more frantic now. I managed to hold off until she came. I followed her instantaneously.

Her tongue now flicking against mine. "Why thank you Seanny."

"Don't call me that"

I spat the words at her. That was what Siobhan had called me in one of her attempts to annoy me.

"Oh sorry, I mean, Sir..."

We lay together on the bed, exhausted. I noticed a saucer caked in ash on top of one of the bookshelves and got up to get my smokes. I lit two, giving one to Elaine as I brought the saucer to the bed. Elaine placed it on her stomach and we smoked in silence until I lit two more.

"Shit, you smoke a lot."

"Got to have one vice, hon."

"Just one? Anyone tell you you're not a half bad fuck?"

"Nope."

"Liar."

I finished my cigarette and lit another. She put on some more music before I turned to her.

"Did anyone ever tell you you give head like you invented it?"

"Everyday."

She took the smoke from my hand taking a drag before I ironically claimed my sexual innocence.

"Yes, Sean..."

This chick never missed a beat and in the most deadpan voice you could imagine furthered the transparently intentional deceit.

"...You do have that virginal look about you, almost prudish."

"You're my first."

"Thought so. You've no technique."

As much as I knew she was joking I started to get that nagging insecurity all men get when they hear these sorts of things.

"You'll have to teach me."

## ●●●●● Chapter Four

Back in the bedsit I was flicking through a Ted Bundy biography. Usual true crime affair. Poorly written but with a few interesting moments. Bundy was always worth reading about. There was something intriguing about his charm and arrogance, how he stole a tree from a mate's house and just walked out of their place without them noticing and drove off in his Beetle with half of it sticking out the roof.

I read about fifty pages, threw it on the bed, stuck on a Velvet Underground record and started thinking about Siobhan. I'd done a lot to forget about the bitch but that wasn't easy. I'd gone out and slept with every variety of woman you could find. Blondes. Brunettes. Black haired. Blue haired. Dyed. Natural. Thin. Fat. And lots of beautiful redheads. They were the hardest to resist. Not that I resisted anyone anyway. I was completely indiscriminate. Couldn't give a shit as long as I got between their legs. And I'd had good ones. Bad ones. Ones who didn't seem to know what they were doing. But it didn't matter. Mostly I was fucking them to kill time. I never met one I liked. One I wanted to spend real time with. One I wanted to talk to. Not since Siobhan. But I had to do something. And they were what I did.

Maybe Elaine would be different but there was about as much hope of that as me shitting a watermelon. But I was glad of that week's work Frank had given me. Not for the 250 but for the amazing fuck that came with it. And shit was it amazing. And I knew it wouldn't be long before I'd be back in her place doing it all over again.

I got out my phone and sent her a text to see if she was free anytime soon. One of those inane "How r u" ones I despised.

Elaine's reply was almost instantaneous.

"i'm gud. hope you enjoyed last nite?"

"v much. wud you like 2 meet again?"

"sure"

"tuesday?"

"gr8"

Fuck I hate text speak. It was another one of those things that had changed. One of those things that made me feel old. And old at 29 for fuck sake! But as long as I got a fuck why would I care what medium, dumbed down as it was, was needed to get one. It was just another necessity.

I'd been half considering inviting Elaine over to the flat but I wasn't sure about it. I'm always a bit wary about letting people know where I live. You never know when they might knock on your door if they do.

Frank seemed to be leaving a shitload of work to me lately. I've no idea what he's been at but working isn't part of it. Still there are worse things than sitting in a room filled with books with Teenage Jesus and The Jerks playing on the stereo. Of course Frank hated when I played any of the No Wave stuff I would become fleetingly obsessed with. "Scares off the customers," he'd told me. But Frank wasn't here so fuck him.

Anyway if they couldn't handle a bit of The Contortions they couldn't handle a good book. And certainly not any of the ones I recommended. Once I'd figured out what they could manage I'd pick something ten times more extreme. Samuel Delaney's *Hogg* was one of my favourites. There was only one copy in the shop and it was mine. I'd keep it under the desk for such special occasions. It was always returned. And the shop would make a profit as there were no refunds.

Of course this did backfire on me every so often. Sometimes it was Frank they returned it to.

"How many times have I told you to stop selling the punters that fucking book? You want to run me out of business?" Frank glared at me but he was hiding a half-smile, "You know if it were anyone else but yourself doing that sort of shite they'd be out on their arses before they knew they'd gotten a kick."

Obviously I'd do it again. And Frank'd give me the same speech over. The thing was I knew Frank got as much of a laugh out of it as I did. He did make a profit out of my little misdeeds after all.

He dragged me out for a drink that evening much to my chagrin. The cunt insisted there'd be no job waiting for me next week if I didn't. We spent an hour and a half drinking pints, Frank throwing back a whiskey with each one. I said my goodbyes to my well pissed boss and hit the road.

•••

"I really don't know what I'm at these days, Sean."

I pulled at a curl in consternation wishing we weren't having this conversation. Not again.

"I'm not exactly the best man to come to looking for advice."

"You seem to have your head fairly well screwed on, look at me wandering around wondering if I should stay in this job or go out and do something worthwhile."

"And what am I doing Kate? Working in a shitty bookshop. Resigned not to bother with any of the things I used to care about. I haven't sang or written anything in years now."

I'm sure the look of ennui was apparent in my eyes. She'd known for a long time I'd given up and I wasn't going to pursue what so many years ago I realised was a lost cause.

"You really should go back to that Sean. You were good. You were more than good. Dublin needed…"

"Dublin didn't care."

"Go somewhere else."

"What? With all those millions of euros I've got hidden under the bed?"

"You could do something."

"I just don't care enough Kate and I can't see that changing. You can do stuff so do it. Write the novel."

She seemed to display a similar sense of resigned desperation as me at this point. Only thing was she could actually achieve the goals she set herself. That is if she stopped talking and actually tried to.

"It's hard, Sean."

"You don't need to leave the job to work on it, do it at night. Shitloads of novelists had to work day jobs, shitloads still do, and they still manage to get stuff out there."

"I know, but it's still hard."

"They'll all tell you that as well, every one of them."

We each lit a cigarette. Kate had this way of needing reassurance. I gave it. Though I was getting tired of it, some days I liked bolstering up Kate's need for recognition. Whether she had the talent or the will to do any of the things she wanted to or not. I didn't know. I would know at some point. I'd know when she got her arse in gear.

"I suppose it's just... I don't know what it is."

"Well I don't know how much that matters really, you're able to do this, I know you are. You're not doomed like me."

"You're not doomed."

"Maybe not, but I tell you I'm fucking bored waiting for Death,"

I said this with a crooked grin still playing with my hair.

"Where is the cunt when you need him?"

"Hear he's busy."

"Fucker always is! Doesn't even go to the right ones half the time. Wish I had his phone number."

"He's a hard one to get. I've tried to Google it a few times. Must be on the fucking dark web."

"You think Death would have a bit more responsibility, wouldn't you?"

"You know yourself, Seanny. The ones with the big jobs, they don't give a shit about the likes of you and me."

And that was how Kate and I spoke.

## ●●●●● Chapter Five

Elaine came into the shop at around four.

"Thought you'd forgotten about me."

"What?"

I attempted to muster as much surprise as I spoke as I was capable of.

"Why would I forget about you?"

I honestly couldn't tell if she was annoyed or taking the piss as she went on.

"Well I haven't heard from you in four days, Mr. Connolly."

"Sorry I meant to send you a text yesterday, I had to see a friend."

"Did you fuck your friend?"

"No, why would you think that?"

"Well…"

Relief. Her tone had switched. It was clear there was no sense of animosity in her words. Where had she taken her acting classes? She was too good at this to have never gone to one.

"…since you could have been fucking me why weren't you?"

Confidence was oozing out of her now. Almost intimidatingly so.

"Well I was hoping we could make up for that bit of lost time tonight."

"Did you now?"

"I was hoping so."

"Well I may give you another chance to rectify your mistake then, Mr. Connolly. Come around at six and forget any plans you have for sleep tonight."

Elaine left and I sat mesmerised. Where the fuck had she come from? Jesus, this chick was different. Fuck.

•••

I was standing on the front step of Elaine's place bang on six and rang the bell. She answered the door in stilettoes, fishnets and a red and black corset. No skirt. No underwear. Her dark bush seeming to greet me.

"Hello Sean, come in."

Once she closed the door I was on my knees licking the patent leather of her shoes and moved up her legs. I was hard already and when I got to her cunt I pulled her down to the floor and fucked her with her legs behind her head. I came hard on top of her. Rolled over and lit a cigarette. She got up and went to the other room returning with a vibrator.

"Ever try one of these?"

"Maybe."

"You don't remember?" A look of consternation on her face.

"I might have been drunk. I've done a lot of things when I've been drunk I can't remember."

"That's a pity."

She was grinning now. It was the most perverse and mischievous grin I'd ever seen. I took it as a good omen for what was to come.

"Yeah?"

"No, not really, because after I'm done you won't say 'maybe' again. You'll have no doubts in your mind about whether you have or whether you haven't. Now get on your knees."

She produced a tub of K.Y. jelly and I presented her my asshole. She inserted it gingerly and turned it on. My cock hard again I started jerking off. She probed inside me trying to find my prostate. After a few near misses which made me feel as if I was getting a medical exam from an inept student doctor she finally hit it. The second it did I almost shot my load there and then. She was right there wasn't going to be any maybe's this time. Once she got the thing where it needed to be she handled it like a pro. Playing with the speed settings. Occasionally turning it off completely. Yeah. She knew what she was doing alright. I felt myself on the verge of orgasm when she pulled it out. She licked the lube and shit dripping from its tip and then replaced the vibrator with her tongue. Eating my asshole as if it was fucking caviar.

I was in ecstasy.

She stopped. Told me to turn over. She got on top and put my cock inside her. She began to spread the rest of the shit that covered her face and mouth over her naked body. She rose and fell violently onto my prick as the beginnings of a lupine scream escaped her mouth eventually filling the room at its crescendo. I came like a machine gun inside her as she continued on to her own climax, dragging her nails down the side of her face as she did so. She looked fucking feral convulsing and howling like that. I was in awe. She tore the stained flesh of her torso with her now broken nails. Spasming on top of me.

When she finally ground to a halt she leaned over close to my face her eyes closed, letting my flaccid prick fall out of her cunt. I could smell my own faecal matter on her skin.

Her eyes shot open; "Now, think you'll remember that?"

## •••••Chapter Six

So what was happening? The months were passing and I was still with Elaine. It was starting to make me feel uncomfortable. I hadn't even started to tire of her yet. She'd even started borrowing my books and I'd started giving her ones for free from the shop. What the fuck was this? Of course I couldn't stop thinking about it. Hard as I tried. And I tried. I could never quite banish the thoughts intruding upon me. Day after day and it began feeling like a kind of torture. If I was a religious man I would have prayed for a reprieve. But I hadn't prayed since I was 6. And it was too late to start now. I'd made up my mind that it was pointless. So I suffered on...

•••

I met Elaine at the gates of Trinity. She asked me what I'd been doing.

"Not much."

"Do you ever do anything?"

"You."

She smiled.

"Want to do that again?"

"As soon as I can."

She grabbed my hand. Brought me up two flights of stairs into an empty lecture hall. She'd gone to college here back in the day and knew the place inside out. We fucked next to the lectern. Then against it. She wasn't wearing underwear. I started to wonder if she ever did.

"Want to go see a film later, Sean?"

"Not particularly."

"Come on! There's some good stuff showing. They're doing a Bergman season in the IFI."

"Alright"

"'Through A Glass Darkly' at six?"

"Ok."

It sounded like a good plan to me. I'd never seen the film on a big screen and it was an offer I was happy to take up.

"Right then, we're going. Want to do anything in between?"

"You."

"We can organise that. Man you really can go for an old guy."

"How old do you think I am? Fucking 70?"

"Joking." She smiled at me. "Sean."

"Well I'm only 69, it hurts my joints at times but I'm fine with the pain."

"So am I."

She sniggered.

"Want to come back to my flat before the film then and I can stick the vibrator up your arse again."

"I was thinking of sticking something up yours."

"We can do that too." She looked at me again. "You sweet old man you."

•••

After we sodomised each other we got ready to leave. Cleaned up all the lube, shit and cum dripping out of us. We got dressed and walked to the cinema. 12 euro in. Each. I paid. Went for a smoke before the flick started. Went in to the darkened screening. Slightly late. Max Von Sydow already in the row boat. Elaine two rows from the back. I sat beside her. She put her hand on my crotch. Didn't rub it this time. I was alright with that. She would later on. So why complain?

The spider/God rape ended the film. I was in desperate need for a smoke. I always get twitchy toward the end of a film. Always try to speed it along with my mind. 90 minutes was a long time without a smoke. More so when you were told you couldn't smoke. So I practically ran to the front door once the credits rolled. Said I'd meet Elaine at the bar. Gave her a twenty euro note. Told her I'd have a coke.

Outside I watched the hipsters pass. I wanted to kill every one of them. I finished my smoke. Lit a second. Smoked it. Threw it to the ground.

We were back in her flat in an hour. Fucking and licking 'til midnight. And then we slept.

I woke to the sound of my phone. Kate at the other end.

"Fancy a coffee?"

"Yeah. When?"

"I'll be free in an hour or so, you be about?"

"Yeah, the usual?"

"Where else?"

"Ok, see you in an hour."

•••

Kate looked well. Kate always looked well. My Bundy bio on the table beside a black coffee and Kate's diet coke.

"Been up to anything Sean?"

"Not much? You?"

"Well, I'm back writing the novel, it's a mess but at least I'm clocking up the words."

"Good to hear."

"How long have you been in this funk, Sean"?

"29 years…"

"Come on, Sean, I'm getting worried about you."

"Don't."

"Can't help it, Sean. You're my friend."

"I'm fine Kate. I'm always fine. When have you not known me to be fine?"

"The last 10 years."

"Don't."

"Sean."

"I said don't, don't say another word, alright, I'm not in the mood and fuck maybe you don't need me as a friend if you're going to worry about me."

"That'd make it worse."

"So I'm supposed to sit here and let you quiz me about being in a funk? I don't need that and you don't need it and it won't do either of us any good."

"Have you ever thought of seeing anyone about it?"

"A prostitute."

"Come on, Sean," she said. "Fuck sake, you're getting predictable."

"When was I not? I need a smoke."

Kate paused then handed me a Camel blue and I walked to the door of the coffee shop. Lit up. Wondered why Kate felt the need to ask these questions. Fuck her anyway, I don't need to answer anything. Don't need to explain myself. My actions. My mood. My fucking mood. Why do people always want to know about my fucking mood? Well they can want all they like but they'll be wanting for a long time. Until I'm dead. Or they are. Either way they'll be waiting.

I went back inside. Kate got up. Went to the door herself.

"So Sean, tell me about this girl."

I sat with my coffee until she came back.

"What girl?"

"Come on Sean, you think I came down in the last hour, you smell of love..." Kate laughed. "Amongst other things."

"Fine. Not much to say. Pretty. Talks a bit too much. Doesn't ask too much though. I like that. You know when people don't ask me too many questions about my personal life. Those types of people can really wreck my head. You know the sort."

"Ah yes, can't stand them myself, the ones always trying to find out your personal business. Hate them."

"And they always tell you it's because they're worried about you."

"Disgusting aren't they?"

"Vile."

"Should be exterminated."

"Most people should be really."

"Think we'd get away with it?"

"Remember years ago how they used to say how there were sites on the internet that told you how to make a bomb?"

"Too easily traced, Sean."

"Maybe, you know anyone with some Zyklon B?"

"Unfortunately not, buuuuuuutttttttttttt I have been working on a formula for Zyklon C."

"That's my girl."

"It's not quite ready yet though."

"Aw Kate, hurry up with it then, I don't know how much longer I can wait."

## ●●●●● Chapter Seven

I wasn't in control. Not in any way. I had no power over the situation at all. None. When it came to Siobhan she was always the dominant one. So I went with it. I was hypnotised. Entranced. I knew she could do this with any man and it was probably my attempts at resistance that made her keep going. And I enjoyed it. Why the fuck shouldn't I?

Post fuck I was smoking a cigarette with a glass of wine on her balcony. I was never allowed smoke inside if she wasn't having one and to be honest I didn't care. As I said she was in control.

"Seanny, why don't you put that out and have your wine inside?"

"Well you know what the man said; drink without smoke is..."

"'...like cock without pussy'. Aren't you a bit old for Bukowski, Sean? Maybe not... I forget you're only 19."

I ignored this.

"Aren't you a bit old for Sylvia Plath?" I'd noticed Plath's collected poems along with The Bell Jar on one of her shelves.

"She knew what she was doing."

"Topping herself you mean?"

"Obviously."

"Always thought she looked like a bad fuck to be honest."

"Of course she was."

"Too much bitching and moaning."

"Don't you like a bitch that moans, Sean?"

"Only in the right context."

"Well that does make sense I suppose. Are you finished that cigarette yet?"

"Yeah, I'll be in in a second."

I put out my smoke and threw back my wine. She filled my glass back up once I lay back down on the bed. She began teasing at my cock.

"Poor thing's worn out maybe I should give him a little kiss and see if that revives him."

"Maybe you should."

She began licking my cock. Between my thighs. My balls. No response.

"Hmmm, he seems very tired."

"Keep going. You might wake him up yet."

"No, I'll leave him be for the moment. We've got a whole night in front of us yet. I want him to be fully prepared."

"You're probably right. Can't expect a man to run a marathon straight after a sprint."

"No, of course not, that would be expecting far too much from any man."

An hour later we were fucking again and continued to for the rest of the night as planned. Sleep was unimportant. Nothing could stop us. Nothing.

•••

Just as I was about to leave the next day she walked over to me and put a copy of de Sade's Justine in my hand.

"Here, read this. I'm getting bored."

"What?"

"Read it."

"I already have."

"Well you had better look at it again... seems as if you've forgotten most of it."

"Fine."

I took the book and left. Fucking bitch. She always had a way of getting at you. She'd never just let you walk out contented she had to get in one last dig before you left. It had been that way since I'd met her in the madhouse two months previously and it didn't matter. Her being three years older than me made me feel like I was being given an education. On love and literature and everything in between.

•••

I was completely in her thrall. I worshipped everything about her. Her mind. Her body. Her wit. The crude X she'd had tattooed in Indian ink over the artery on her left wrist so she knew where to cut if she wanted to.

Her world was the one I wanted to live in. I'd never known anything like it before. Never known anyone like *her* before. And it was bliss.

I kept going to the groups. Found out the short haired chick's name was Julianne. Found out a lot about her. That is, of course, if she were telling the truth. She didn't seem to have the brain capacity to do anything other than that though. I continued lying. Continued talking about my fictional dead father and the smell of his flesh. These fuckers weren't going to learn anything more than they needed to know, which was nothing. Me speaking was all they wanted. The more tragic the tale I spun the better.

I don't know why I kept going. Maybe some sort of masochistic impulse that had been lying dormant inside my psyche? It didn't matter. The groups were the only part of my life that was any different than before. Them and Elaine. Two opposite situations. Maybe it was balance I was after. I didn't give it much thought.

•••

It was Elaine's flat tonight. It had been her flat all day.

"What's wrong?"

"Nothing."

"Sean, tell me."

"There's nothing the fuck wrong. Why should there be anything fucking wrong. What does it matter? I'm here. We'll fuck. What else do you need? You wouldn't like to hear what goes on in my head. I tell you that Elaine. You wouldn't want to hear it."

"Why not?"

"Maybe I want to kill you. Maybe I'm sick of you. Maybe you should fuck off."

Instant regret.

"Or at least just leave me be. Sometimes I get like this. Am I not allowed get like this? My thoughts are my own alright. I don't want anyone probing around. Groping them. Trying to understand them. Nobody can or will. That's how I like it. And that's how it's going to stay."

"Jesus, Sean. I was just wondering."

"Well don't. Don't fucking wonder. It's best that way alright? Best for both of us. So just shut up. Just shut the fuck up."

Elaine had never heard me speak with that sort of venom before and she looked shocked.

"Ok, ok, I will."

We didn't fuck that night and I didn't sleep.

●●●

I didn't even bother waking her when I left. Instead put on my clothes and just got the fuck out. Walked toward Baggot Street.

"Hey bud."

I turned to see a scumbag in a hoodie and grey tracksuit bottoms.

"What?!"

"Relax bud, I only wanted to ask you something?"

I don't know why the fuck I didn't keep walking. Maybe it was because if I stayed I could split his head open against a fucking wall.

"Yeah?"

"You got the price of a hostel?"

"No. You got any gear?"

"Keep it quiet would you... here, let's go for a chat."

"Fine..."

"So you're looking?"

"No, now fuck off!"

"No bother, come down here, I'll sort you."

And I felt the blade. The cunt was quick. I'll give him that.

"Your wallet, please. And if you fucking say a fucking word you're fucking dead... right?"

I gave him the wallet. Only a 20 inside. He looked.

"Is this all you fucking have, cunt?"

I said yeah and got a bang of his fist to the side of the head. Kick to the balls. I was on my knees now. Another kick. This time to the head. I was flat on the ground. A few more in the ribs. And the dealer whispered;

"A pleasure bud... anytime you need a bit more a that give us a shout."

He ran.

I lay on the ground for a long time before picking himself up. I went home shaking.

## ●●●●● Chapter Eight

I didn't go outside for a week after that. Just walked around with the lights off listening to The Velvets' White Light/White Heat.

I rang Elaine. Apologised for the stupid fight. Told her what had happened.

"Fuck!"

"Yeah..."

My voice was barely audible down the phone.

"You alright, Sean?"

I didn't answer. She was over within an hour. Sat with me on the floor. Didn't ask any questions. Just sat and listened to the special edition white vinyl Velvets' album with me. Turned it over for me when it needed to be. I'd told her I couldn't listen to anything else. She didn't mind.

Elaine was alright. She just wanted to look after me. That was alright. A chick who wanted to look after you. Well... in a way. There were worse things she could have been doing. She could have been asking me questions. She could have been talking. I didn't want to talk. I didn't want to answer questions. I just wanted to listen to The Velvets and lie in bed.

I considered going down to one of the pawn shops on Thomas Street. Getting myself a knife. Finding the bastard and slitting his fucking throat. One more dead scumbag wouldn't bother the cops. But how the fuck was I going to find him? They all looked the same. And in the haze of the night my mind had glossed over what his face looked like anyway. No. That was pointless. So I just kept quiet. Listened. Eventually I was able to leave the bedsit again. Even fuck Elaine again. But that all took time. Two weeks to leave. Four to fuck.

•••

Siobhan looked at me with those green eyes that always made me feel as if she knew every thought I'd ever had. We were lying on the couch. Me looking like an anorexic Robert Smith, her a "Wait Until Dark" period Audrey Hepburn.

"Have you ever read Hobbes, Seanny?"

"I haven't actually, been meaning to get round to him."

"Do you know what he says about life?"

"Tell me."

She was still staring. Should I know this?

"That it's nasty brutish and short."

I put my arm around her.

"Sounds about right. Not short enough though."

"Well that's a matter of choice now isn't it?"

•••

I hadn't gone into work for a while. Elaine had gotten in touch with Frank. Told him what had happened. Frank was alright about it. Didn't try to push me. He knew better than to do that. Knew I'd just walk out.

Thing that worried me was that someone would make the suggestion I go back into the madhouse. I couldn't afford cigarettes. My money wasn't going anywhere else but I still couldn't afford 30 quid a day.

Fucking a chick with a job did have its upsides. A few actually. At that moment though that was the main one. I needed cigarettes more than air.

## •••••Chapter Nine

After a few weeks attending the group I'd decided to make a move on Julianne. It didn't take me long to get her into bed. I'd known she'd be easy. I arranged to meet her outside the group. We'd have a drink. We'd talk. We'd flirt. We might fuck but I wasn't holding out for that on the first night.

We met in one of those upscale places in Temple Bar. The type of place I usually hate. The ones that are filled with people who feel the need to saturate themselves with their status. Julianne came in in a short green dress. Hair perfect. Too much make up. We had two drinks and I could see she was ready. Ready to dispense with them. Get to wherever the fuck she lived. Get my cock inside her. It seemed we'd the same plan from the beginning and I wasn't going to complain.

She seemed to moan less outside the group and it had surprised me. I found it hard to believe she could actually shut that off but somehow she did. We drank. Got a bit pissed. Got into a cab. Went to her apartment. One of those D4 gated communities.

When we got out of the taxi she keyed in a code. The gate opened. We walked to the entrance. She keyed in another code and we got in a lift. Then we were in her apartment drinking fancy red wine. No plastic corks for Julianne. Too common. I could tell this bitch had never worked a day in her life. Mammy and Daddy had paid her way since she blighted this earth.

●●●

She wasn't a bad fuck. Not a great one. Nothing like Elaine. Like everything else in her life she obviously had never put any effort into it. She could move. There was a flexibility to her and little else. Those fucks are hard to remember, like all mediocre things.

I came. Asked for more wine. Threw it back. Slept in her place that night. Wondering if I'd see her again. I hoped not. I needed to fuck her to get rid of the feeling that she was anything like Siobhan. She wasn't and I stopped going to the groups.

About a month later I met Paul on Camden St.

"Sean, how are you?"

This was odd. Nobody was supposed to greet anybody else outside the group due to confidential nature of what was talked about there. I stopped and greeted him.

"Hi, Paul."

"Do you want to get a coffee, Sean?"

"Well, I'm in a bit of a rush to be honest, Paul," I eyed him but couldn't work him out. He just looked at me. "But I'd prefer a pint either way."

"Ok, let's go in here."

We went into one of the hipster places that line Camden St. and I ordered us a round. I brought over the drinks, sat with Paul.

"I've a bit of bad news, Sean."

"Yeah?"

"You remember Julianne?"

"The one with the short black hair? Yeah, of course."

"She died three weeks ago."

Fuck. I hadn't expected this. She couldn't have, she didn't have the guts.

"What happened?"

Paul winced.

"It was suicide, Sean." He tried to lock my eyes. "I'm sorry to have to tell you like this. Everyone in the group was pretty devastated when we heard the news but since you'd stopped coming I couldn't tell you."

No shit, Paul.

"When I saw you I couldn't just walk by. I'm really sorry. It's really a tragedy."

"How... how'd she do it, Paul?"

"Well I wasn't told that, Sean." He drew a card out of his pocket. "If you want to talk to me about it anytime, day or night, call me."

I started twisting my hair. Fidgety. Needing to get away from him.

"I... I've got to go alright? I'll ring you ok?"

Paul looked like he was going to come out with one of his usual platitudes but thankfully he restrained himself.

"Of course you're and welcome back to the group anytime but I can understand if you don't want to, a lot of people left after we heard."

"Shit, well thanks for telling me..."

"Ok, Sean."

I downed my pint and half stumbled home. Fuck!

Fuck! Fuck! Fuck!

On my way home I bought a cheap bottle of wine and dropped some Ativan. I fell into a dreamless sleep. The last I can remember.

## ●●●●●Chapter Ten

After I'd gotten back on my feet things were different. Between me and Elaine I mean. We'd become something else. Something strange. Closer maybe. Different anyway. We didn't fuck as much though when we did it was still as good as it ever was. We talked more. Talked about other things rather than just books and movies. I no longer hid my disgust at the world from her and neither did she hide her warped optimism. She reckoned there was a way we could make our way through this vile mess of a life somehow satisfied with ourselves. I didn't argue but didn't agree either. It was a nice thought but an implausible one all the same.

I realised I was actually enjoying myself for once.

It wouldn't last.

It didn't last.

The whole debacle with Julianne made Siobhan start to present herself in a more definite manner than she'd had before and soon I was with her more and more.

Elaine began to melt into the background, Siobhan soon sitting at the foot of my bed for hours on end just looking at me. Her wrist bloodied. A mute witness to a crime I didn't commit. Why now? Why was she doing this now? It'd been ten years. I'd gotten rid of her for the most part after her second anniversary. It'd taken a lot. Drink. Drugs. Extra therapy.

Thankfully Grace had never sent me to another one of those groups after it'd happened. I had to give her her due for that. She wasn't a total fucking idiot. She knew when to stop. Knew that if she sent me back she mightn't see me again. And I think she actually liked our sessions in some perverse way. I challenged her which I could tell from the blank faces of those I saw in the waiting room was not something that happened every day. What a sad existence she must lead. Particularly since she was supposed to be an advocate of the good life. She couldn't be seen to be like me though who knows what she was really like?

## ●●●●● Chapter Eleven

In work one Monday there was a chick loitering in one of the corners. She came up to the till with some Anais Nin and a biography of e.e. cummings I hadn't read. I couldn't believe I hadn't spotted it when I came in. It was an old one and I wasn't going to get a chance to read it now. Another missed opportunity...

I asked her for five quid and as she handed it over what I saw on her wrist made my face blanch. It was Siobhan. No, no, all those bitches from that part of town looked the same. But, fuck, she was the spit of her. And it was the sort of thing Siobhan would do. It was just how life was with me. Seeing someone just to remind me of all I'd been trying to forget since back then.

I put the Siobhan lookalike's books in a brown paper bag without saying a word. She thanked me and left. The room began to close in on me. I had to get out.

It was a perfectly normal reaction to believe you've seen or think you've seen someone you once knew who's since passed on. But I'd only been back in work a week. I wasn't prepared for this sort of shit.

Then came the voice;

"Hello Sean."

This time it wasn't a lookalike. This time it was her. I couldn't say anything.

"Long time no see." She was talking as if she'd only been away for a month. Not ten years.

"Why aren't you, you know, talking?"

I still didn't answer.

"What did you think I was actually, like, dead or something?"

She was as beautiful and contemptuous as I'd always remembered her to be.

"Sean... when what happens to me happens, you, well... you get a little perspective."

"Right."

"I've just come back up. Wanted to see how my favourite little murderer was doing."

Again I couldn't answer.

"You don't think you're a murderer then? Come now Seanny, you know you are."

I stuttered and said I wasn't.

"Oh dear, don't you remember what happened? Poor thing you."

She took a pen from her bag and gently took hold of my wrist which I immediately jerked away.

"What? Bad memories? Well this is where..."

She drew an X on my wrist.

"...my tattoo was and this is what you told me to do."

She took another pen from her bag and drew a line up my arm.

"Then you took a piece of glass and stuck it in, remember now? Well if that isn't murder Seanny I don't know what is."

"It wasn't... I didn't do that."

She smiled.

"Ok Seanny whatever you want to think, I'll be seeing you around. Quite a lot I think."

She turned and walked out the door as beautiful as ever and I felt the room begin to spin.

What had just happened?

I lay on my back and watched the ceiling for half an hour. I couldn't move. I was completely paralysed and my brain was going haywire. What the fuck could I do? I mean fuck this made no sense but it seemed really than anything I'd ever experienced before.

## ●●●●● Chapter Twelve

I got out of the shop fast. Shaking. Just about able to lock the door and ran to the nearest place I could get a drink. I ordered a whiskey and a pint. Downed the whisky before taking the pint outside. I started chaining the cigs I'd bought that morning. Soon most of the pack was gone. There was fuck all left of the pint either.

I didn't have the cash for another pack of straights considering the amount of alcohol I knew I'd need.

"Fuck," I thought to myself, "I hope Frank doesn't find out."

He'd freak if he knew I'd closed the place early. Maybe he'd understand though I was playing a dodgy game. Frank was understanding but he couldn't keep me on if I was going to lose him business. He wasn't running a charity and I knew that. But that was what I needed, fucking charity.

I got myself to another spot where I could get a pint for a reasonable price. I ordered another whiskey and a pint. I'm sure I looked like shit. The barman didn't look overly enthusiastic to serve me. Fuck him I thought, I'm paying the fucker's wages. Still I dropped the J.D. when I went up again and just got another pint. And then another. And another. And so on.

I was obviously wrong about the barman's feelings toward me. I went home and fell asleep.

I woke up at 8pm and started again. No worries about getting served in the local. The staff there would give me a drink if I walked in on bloody stumps. And that's how I *did* feel when I got there. As if I had been mutilated. Lacerated by memories of that stupid bitch who *had* deserved to die. Needed to. But what the fuck was this? I needed to block it out. And I fucking well did.

When I got back to the bedsit Elaine was asleep. Elaine was asleep. Tripped over her shoes. Got undressed. Got into bed beside her. She was naked and I put my arm around her. Left hand on her right breast. I couldn't believe this was happening. Life was actually going well for me recently. Mostly anyway. What with Elaine around and everything things were actually half decent. So why the fuck would Siobhan come back after two years? There was no explanation for it. No explanation other than the world was trying to fuck me over. Again. It was fond of that. Obviously she resented Elaine. Or that I had found someone like Elaine. And Elaine. Well. Elaine was the only light left. The only thing that made life worth living. She was a saint. And this shithole needed one. Needed one badly. And Elaine was that saint. Fuck Siobhan. I was holding onto Elaine. No matter what. No fucking Demiurge was going to take her away. No old memories. Nothing.

*Saint of the City*

I couldn't believe this was happening. Life was actually going well for me recently. Mostly anyway. What with Elaine around and everything things were actually half decent.

So why the fuck would Siobhan come back after five years? There was no explanation for it. No explanation other than the world was trying to fuck me over. Again. It was fond of that.

Obviously she resented Elaine. Or that I had found someone like Elaine. And Elaine. Well. Elaine was the only light left. The only thing that made life worth living. She was a saint. And this shithole needed one. Needed one badly. And Elaine was that saint.

Fuck Siobhan. I was holding onto Elaine. No matter what. No fucking Demiurge was going to take her away. No old memories. Nothing.

Elaine's hair was wet and she was wearing nothing but my dressing gown. She'd gotten out of the shower, laid down and drifted off.

I undid my belt and straddled her. Her eyes opened. She smiled.

"Hello, Sir."

"Shut up, bitch."

"Yes Sir."

I undid the dressing gown and pumped my cock hard until I came on her tits. She licked the remaining spunk off the tip of my cock.

"Well thank you, Sir." She rubbed the glob I'd spilled across her over the rest of her torso, sort of undulating, sort of stretching and said: "I must say I enjoyed that."

I collapsed onto the mattress beside her.

"I love you, Sean."

I laid there for a minute.

"I love you, Elaine."

## •••••Chapter Thirteen

I remember the night. Fuck, I remember it too well and it wasn't the way she was saying it'd been. Me and Siobhan had gotten shitfaced within an hour on expensive wine and she'd began talking about suicide.

The wine had long gone to our heads but we kept drinking. Siobhan was still talking about suicide and I was starting to worry. After another bottle she broke a glass and placed it on the X on her wrist. I jumped up.

"Stop! What the fuck are you doing!"

"Oh come on Seanny, what's the point?"

She was crying now.

"No, stop, you're drunk, please."

"We could do it together Seanny, leave this place behind and sail off into eternity."

"No we're not going to do that, stop, please."

She dropped the piece of glass and I put my arms around her. We were both crying now. I took her into the bedroom and we got under the covers. I held her until I passed out.

•••

The next morning I woke up in an empty bed and painfully hungover. I had no idea where Siobhan was and immediately a surge of adrenaline hit me. I went into the sitting room and that's where I found her.

That was what happened. It didn't happen the way she said it did. I know that's how it happened. I swear I know.

•••

"I'm afraid of losing Elaine."

As always Grace's beautiful legs were on display. Crossed but inviting. Begging to be parted. Her hungry cunt asking to be fucked.

"Why do you think that, Sean?"

"I'm not sure... but I need her now. I'm worried, fuck, I don't know what I'm worried about."

"You haven't had it easy recently, Sean."

"Ah for fuck sake, Grace, I've had it just as easy as I've ever had it. Everything's been a mess since Siobhan died."

I hadn't meant to bring that up.

"You've managed to hold down a job... you seem to have your drinking under control."

"Most of the time."

"Sean, it used to be a lot worse. You've learned a lot since we started seeing each other."

Why was I doing this?

"Listen... I wouldn't mind leaving it at that for the minute."

"If you're sure, Sean."

To someone else her voice may have sounded benign but I knew it was just another line. I'd heard it too many times.

"I don't want you leaving concerned about something which I don't think you should worry too much about."

All in my head is it, Grace? All in my fucking head?

"It's just I'm a bit anxious today. I'd prefer to come back to it next week or something."

"Ok, Sean, that's no problem at all."

I left Grace's having gained nothing except another fantasy of Grace.

I walked for a while. I'd been doing this a lot more since Siobhan had re-entered my mind. Completely occupying it at times. How was I supposed to get rid of her? Go to a fucking priest?

I took a stroll through one of the nearby parks and had a good look at all the thirty-something mothers and au pairs. They were always a good distraction. I hoped Elaine would be in the flat when I got back. She'd moved in to help me out with the rent and considering she was spending more time in my place than she was in hers.

I couldn't count on Elaine being there, though. She had work. She had friends. She had a lot of things unnecessary to survival. Maybe a job was important but friends? Who the fuck needed friends and I couldn't stand a single one of hers. They all seemed like idiots to me so whenever she talked about meeting them I'd tell her it was important she spend some time away from me and have a little independence. Now I wondered if they might be filling her with poison. Telling her to get rid of me. Find someone more sociable. More well-adjusted. Fuck, I couldn't figure a way to get rid of them though. I thought there must be some way but the answer to eluded me.

I'd figure it out, though.

## •••• Chapter Fourteen

Siobhan smiled a sort of idiot grin and placed my cock inside her wet pussy. She took the full tip of my shaft inside her and then lifted herself off within a few seconds. She got off me and started sucking. I came almost immediately. She rose to meet my eye and spat my cum in my face. She leaned back and started masturbating caressing her left breast as she did so. I could see the deep gash down the inside of her arm where she'd inserted the blade at her wrist and brought it to near her elbow.

"Killed anyone else recently, Sean?"

"What?"

"I asked if you've killed anyone else?"

"No! Fuck off! I didn't kill you anyway!"

"No? You sure Sean? You sure you didn't kill me?"

"I fucking well didn't, you bitch. You killed yourself!"

"Ah ok, I'd… hmmm…. forgotten… sorry… you know you're going to kill her don't you?"

"Who? What the fuck are you talking about?"

I tried to move but her thighs pinned me to the bed. Even with her hand violently massaging her clit she was able to hold me.

"That sweet little Elaine… ah… emmm… you're going to kill her Sean…ah…"

"No I'm not you fucking bitch." I wanted out from beneath her. I couldn't understand what was happening and how the fuck could I?

"Get the fuck off me Siobhan!"

"Oh, not yet Sean..." Her voice. That voice of hers. It was so soft and seductive yet it veiled a menace.

"Don't you want to see a dead girl cum?"

"GET OFF ME YOU FUCKING CUNT!"

She leaned her face close to mine moaning. Her lizard's tongue darted from her lips and she let out a scream.

"NOW! SEAN! NOW! YES! NOW MAKE HER SEAN! MAKE HER LIKE THIS SEAN! NOW SSSSEEEEAAAANNNNN!"

## ●●●●● Chapter Fifteen

Elaine looked concerned.

"What were you dreaming about?"

My voice was weak and husky but that was usual. "Fuck… I don't know. Was I talking in my sleep?"

"That'd be putting it mildly…" Elaine laughed. "You were practically screaming."

"What did I say?"

"I couldn't make much out apart from you telling someone to 'fuck off'."

"Must have been about Frank…"

I forced a grin. Elaine leaned over to give me a kiss. I shirked.

"You sure you're ok?"

"Yeah, I'm grand. Could you pass me the cigs?"

Elaine got the pack of cigarettes from the bedside table. The lighter. The ashtray. I lit one. Offered one to her.

"No, I'm going to have a tea first. You want a coffee?"

She eased her way out of the bed and walked naked across the room to the kettle, filled it with water and set it back down to boil.

"I'm alright for the minute," I didn't feel comfortable saying this. "Shit, I wonder what I was dreaming about."

I could practically still feel Siobhan's breath on my face. Thighs on my waist. Tongue on my mouth.

"Dreams are strange things..." She was trying to be reassuring but it came out as condescending.

"You know all that Freud stuff was nonsense?"

"Yeah, I know. I'm in therapy Elaine. For years."

She must have realised the offensive nature of her remark and immediately apologised.

"Shut up, Elaine, you know it's alright."

"Yeah, but you don't look too good Sean. When are you seeing Grace next?"

"Thursday, I think."

She took a cigarette from the pack on the bed and lit it.

"You find her any good?"

"I'm just awake, Elaine."

"Well, fuck it, you're always a grumpy fucker. When should I ask you? When would you tell me?"

"You mightn't want to know what I've to tell."

"Really."

"Savage fucking legs, minute I sit down she flashes me a little more thigh. Tell you hon, one day I'm going to go in and she's just going to ride me on my chair."

This eased any of the tension that had that was left and it's was clear she was comfortable again. In the clear.

"Fuck off you bollocks, you sure you don't want a coffee?"

"No, I'm grand hon, seriously, thanks though."

She back into bed with her tea and her cigarette, taking the ashtray from me and balancing it on her hip.

"Give me a kiss before I take a shower, you might be asleep by the time I get out of it."

I did.

●●●

I stayed in the flat most of the day. Walking in circles and scratching my bollocks. I couldn't read more than a couple of pages at a time. Didn't even have a wank. Just arsed around and smoked. Agitated. I took some extra Valium which failed to relieve any of the anxiety and I didn't particularly want to take too many more or I'd have run out way before my next script was due. Fuck it I thought to myself, I'll get some wine. That'll do the job for a bit anyway.

I got the wine. Tried to block out the dream but it kept coming back. Why would I kill Elaine? I fucking loved Elaine. I could no more kill Elaine than I would kill Michel Houelbecq and I certainly had no intentions of doing that. The dream made no sense. Stress. That's all. A stress dream. Nothing more. Fuck though it was a nasty bastard of a one.

## ••••• Chapter Sixteen

Myself and Elaine were sitting in The Udolfo. I thought she might appreciate going back there. It was nice to see her decked out in all her finery again, wearing the fishnets and heels that had always driven me mad.

"We should do this more often, Sean. God I don't know when the last time we were here."

"Yeah, it's been awhile alright."

"How was Grace this week?"

"The usual."

"She jump you?"

"Tried but I fended her off."

"Good boy."

The godawful music that was the norm in The Udolfo was playing as the drinks started going down more quickly. I hadn't noticed until I was getting up to order a round and saw that Elaine was only halfway through her pint. She waved me off. Said go ahead. On the way back I noticed a slight disequilibrium in my gait. It didn't put me off. I was now that one drink past caring. I'd doubled up on whisky by the time we were outside looking for a cab. And I was stumbling properly by that point.

Elaine wasn't impressed as she started to get ready for bed when we got back.

"I'm not fucking going back to that stupid fucking place. It's a fucking shithole... all those pathetic cunts trying to look cool."

My words were half formed as they came out.

"Fine, Sean, we don't have to go again."

"Like the place was shit, the music was shit, the drinks were shit, everything about the place was shit."

"Fine, Sean! Just get into bed would you?"

"No, I mean, like, I only went to there the first time so I could fuck..."

My eyes shot open. Wider than I ever remember them opening before. In the corner Siobhan sat naked masturbating.

She whispered: "Keep going Seanny, you're going to do it soon, come on Seanny, keep going."

"Fuck off, you bitch!"

"What the fuck, Sean? What was that in aid of? We don't have to go to The Udolfo again, alright? I just asked you to get into bed."

I looked at Siobhan again. She seemed like she was close to cumming.

"Go on, Seanny..."

"FUCK OFF!"

Elaine noticed I wasn't looking at her.

"Sean, what the fuck's up?"

I just kept looking at Siobhan. Shouting. Screaming. Telling her to fuck off.

Last thing I remember I was hugging the toilet puking my ring up.

## •••••Chapter Seventeen

I woke shaking with a cunt of a headache. Elaine was across the room looking at me.

"Are you ok?"

"Just about."

"Shit, Sean, you were in bits last night,"

He face flushed with concern

"You really scared me. I had to call a doctor and everything."

"What? A doctor?"

"Well, it couldn't have been alcohol that did that to you so I thought you might have gotten your drink spiked."

I wasn't sure how to respond to this.

"Once I'd told the doctor you'd been sick he said you'd probably gotten most of the toxins out of your system but to keep an eye on you today. Do you remember anything?"

Once again my words weren't coming out too well. "Not much."

"The doctor said that you should rest, I just have to go out and get us some milk but I'll be back in a minute, ok?"

"Yeah, no problem."

Elaine left and I lay there.

Laid there remembering Siobhan. Remembering her naked body. Her hand on her cunt. Taunting me. Telling me to do something I would never do. Saw her writhe. Her face contort. Her lips spitting poison. I could smell her cunt. I could smell it in the room. It lingered as a reminder she'd been here.

I closed my eyes.

We were fucking. She'd come in shortly after Elaine had left and mounted me. Her hands were around my throat. And fuck she was good. She'd gotten better. Her hips moving wildly. Her legs pumping. Her eyes like a demon's.

She got the belt that was lying beside us and wrapped it around my neck without breaking her rhythm. I was getting closer.

"Maybe you should do it this way, Sean? Kill her this way? It might be quicker? Kinder?"

I didn't respond. Couldn't respond. The belt was too tight.

"Yes, Sean, I think it might be a nice way for her to go."

Siobhan leaned back and screamed as she orgasmed closing the belt even tighter. I didn't know how much longer I had to live but I knew I wasn't going to be taken now. Not by Siobhan. Not until I killed Elaine. I came furiously inside Siobhan nearly blacking out from the surge of ecstatic pleasure.

"Yes, Sean..."

I opened my eyes. Elaine was back. She looked at and through me. She must have seen fucking fear in my eyes.

"Do you want a coffee, Sean?"

I told her I was alright and I'd be fine on my own for a while. I didn't know what I was supposed to do. Didn't know if I'd ever be let rest. I could feel the damp from where I'd cum in my sleep. Where I'd cum in Siobhan.

I didn't want Elaine to smell Siobhan. Smell her sweat. Her hideous cunt. I couldn't let Elaine know that she'd been here. That she'd only just left.

She couldn't ever know. I wouldn't let that happen. And Siobhan was dangerous. I knew it well. I knew that if I didn't kill Elaine it would only be a matter of time before Siobhan would.

I had to protect Elaine. I just didn't know how to.

## ●●●●● Chapter Eighteen

Siobhan was in the room again. She was talking. Talking about Elaine. How it must be done. Of course she was naked as always. She started to suck me off. Siobhan had always given great head. Mind blowing head. I hate to say it but she made Elaine look like an amateur. And there was nothing I could do but lie back and enjoy it. I was beyond resisting now. Way beyond it.

She suggested the belt again. How it would be quick. But she suggested many things. Pouring bleach down her throat. Cutting her open. Maybe even opening her wrists as she insisted I'd done to her. That was bullshit of course. Siobhan had done that herself. I may have shown her how but she'd done it herself.

Siobhan never ceased to say otherwise though. To say I held the broken glass against the X on her wrist. Dragged it up to her elbow. She was relentless with this and I had stopped bothering to defend myself. She was always deluded. There was no way I could shake her out of it and I never had been able to in the past.

"Fuck it," I thought to myself, "just let it go man."

What did it matter now? The only important thing now was to keep her away from Elaine. If letting her suck me off and ignoring her lies then so be it. Elaine was my priority. And would remain so.

*Saint of the City*

Siobhan had been following me everywhere and any chance she got she'd take me aside for a fuck. I say she followed me but it was more like she appeared in front of me. Always in the same way. No clothes and ready to fuck. She'd pull me aside in work, open my trousers and ride me on the floor. Or blow me beneath the cash register as I served customers. I was rarely alone.

The only time I got any peace was when Elaine was around. When I was with Elaine there was never any sign of Siobhan. Though it was a relief to be rid of her for a few hours I never knew what she might be doing. Where she might be. She could be waiting outside the door for all I knew. Could be fucking anywhere. Could be waiting to get Elaine by herself. That was the good thing about when she was with me. I knew she wasn't doing anything to Elaine. I was not committing any infidelity by fucking her. I was keeping Elaine alive.

I hadn't a notion how to stop Siobhan from whatever she might do otherwise. So I fucked her as much as I could. Kept her in full view whenever possible. But, of course, I couldn't do that 24 hours a day and that terrified me. She was fucking insane after all. It was obviously her who'd spiked my drink in The Udolfo. Who else would waste good drugs on a stranger? The answer was self-evident. Nobody. Nobody except Siobhan would do that. She knew I'd see her when I'd hallucinate. Knew she was in the forefront of my mind. She truly was an insidious bitch. She'd known I was dreaming of her too. Of course she fucking did.

## •••••Chapter Nineteen

"Hello, stranger."

There were a few customers in. Siobhan never talked when there were people in the place. She hid then. I turned around to see Kate.

"Fuck! How are you?"

It was rare that Kate would drop into the shop like this. She really must have been bored and I didn't have the time and I was too preoccupied for boredom now nor for conversation. But I had to fake it. She'd be gone soon so I capitulated.

"Not bad, this woman of yours not letting you see me anymore?"

"Could you blame her?"

"Few could."

"There's your answer."

"Ah well, better do it in secret from now on."

"Sounds like a plan, alright."

"Well I'm a woman who's always got a plan, lots of them in fact."

"Don't I know it...?"

"You up for a pint once you're done?"

"Maybe a quick one..."

I had to get home because I couldn't leave Elaine alone and I couldn't tell Kate that. I'd go for the drink and split as soon as I could. She'd wonder what was going on but I couldn't give a shit what Kate wondered about. Never had to be honest so fuck her.

"Right, Sean boy, what time you off?"

"About an hours' time."

"See you down in Brogans then..."

We met. We drank. We talked. Talked for too long in my opinion. I wanted to get back to Elaine. Kate kept throwing drinks at me and there was nothing else I could do but drink them. Maybe I needed it. Needed to calm down. Yeah, I suppose I did. I let myself think for a second I was overreacting about all this. That Siobhan would never go near Elaine. She wanted me not her. Wanted to fuck me up. But then maybe the best way to do that was to get at Elaine.

Fuck! No, I wasn't overreacting. I needed to get back.

I downed my drink. Told Kate I had to go.

"What's the rush, Sean?"

I bit my tongue at first: "Got to do something."

She fucking sneered back: "Someone you mean?"

"Fuck you Kate, go back to your shitty little pretensions of being a fucking artist. I couldn't be fucking arsed listening to you sit here and spout your shit anymore. Some of us actually *do* what we set out to do so go fucking do it. You fucking need to spend less time fucking talking to me and more time working right! Actually don't fucking talk to me again until you've done something right? Don't fucking come near me!"

Elaine was having a smoke when I got back. I took it out of her hand. Threw it into the ash tray and kissed her. Tore off her underwear and started fucking her. With each thrust I just kept thinking to myself: "You're safe hon, you're safe with me, no one's going to hurt you. No one..."

## •••••Chapter Twenty

"You ok Sean? You seem a little, I don't know, off."

"I'm fine, hon."

"You sure?"

"I'm fine, alright? Nothing wrong with me."

"Fair enough."

"Just leave me be, alright? You don't need to worry about me. Ever."

"I can't help that. You don't have a say in it either."

"Ah, fuck it for a bit and let me get on with things."

"Sean! For fuck's sake."

"Well at least don't ask me about it. That just makes it worse ok?"

She looked at me and I looked away.

"I've got to get off. Frank's doing fuck all these days. Seems like he's on a permanent holiday recently."

"He giving you anything extra?"

"Not much, but enough."

"Better than nothing, I suppose."

Thankfully it was busy that day. No Siobhan. Elaine safe in work. Me surrounded by book buyers and browsers. The browsers probably the best read of them all. Never asking stupid questions. The only problem with them was they took up room and could be looking round the place for well over an hour without putting anything in the till. That meant there was nothing for me to take from the till. At least they understood the function of the place and anyone who came in regularly would pick something up by the end of the week knowing the place wasn't a fucking bus shelter.

Today's folk were the sort you needed in a place like this. And I was happy. No, not happy. That's too strong a word. I was ok with them. No one asking me anything. No one looking for discounts... which meant they got discounts. A fair bit of stock left the building before closing time so that was a few extra quid for me on Friday. A bookseller on commission. It was an unlikely position but it was bonus money that was all. The few pints Frank got me most weeks would be enough for most so working on commission wasn't a particularly bad thing.

Come six though I was itching to get back to Elaine though I was never permitted to shoo the customers out. And it would have been stupid of me to do so anyway. I needed all the cash I could get but you can always tell a browser from a buyer. Different look to them. Something in the eyes. Or the mouth. Or the thighs. Something anyway.

At six-ten, this bitch came in. It was pissing rain outside. She didn't even look at the books. Didn't even make any effort at pretence. Just stood inside the door trying to talk to me about the weather. I was about two seconds from telling the bitch to buy something or get the fuck out when she left. Couldn't believe it.

There were only three reasons to come in. To buy. To browse. Or to fucking suck me off.

She didn't fulfil any of these requirements.

A book to the head was coming her way.

Bitch was lucky.

## ●●●●● Chapter Twenty One

I decided to stop working in the shop. Leaving Elaine alone was too risky. It was better for her if I stayed home. Watched her when she got home. The pittance Frank gave me every week wasn't worth it. I was still getting my dole and rent allowance and Elaine threw in an every quid towards that. Whatever bit of luxury those extra few euro were giving it was nothing to keeping Elaine safe. I knew I'd have Siobhan to deal with until while I waited but she wouldn't break me.

Not a fucking chance. She mightn't ever fuck off but I could handle her. I knew I could. She was only a bitch toy I played with once. Nothing more. Nothing.

I was lying to myself, of course. She was far more than that. She was a manipulative homicidal whore who wanted her revenge. And revenge for what? Revenge for something so fucking inconsequential, so inevitable. Nobody blamed me for it except her. Everyone else was on my side. I left her. So what? I drew a little mark on her wrist. Who cared? Just her. That's all. And me.

She had never been trustworthy. Even when we had been going out I was never sure what I'd come back to. If I'd have to ring an ambulance. If I'd have to wrap a tourniquet around one of her arms or legs. If I'd have to stay up all night to make sure she didn't go and take all her fucking pills at once. It was constant. Never a break. I was always on alert for that sort of shit. It wasn't fair and it wasn't fair what she was doing to me now. All I'd done was help her like I had every other day. I couldn't keep that up. Couldn't be expected to keep it up. And who would say otherwise?

The only thing easy about Siobhan was getting her legs open. Everything else was a struggle.

But I kept at it until I couldn't do it anymore. And now she was torturing me because of it. She really was an evil bitch. I knew she'd keep at it and I had no way to stop her. There was no way to stop her.

So what to do? Grin and bear it? Seemed so. Just like I had when I had been going out with her. A lover spurned. That's what she was. And how do you sort that out? Kill her? I couldn't do that. I couldn't have her blood on my hands like I'd once thought I'd had. No. There must be another way. Any free time I had I tried to figure out a way.

Thing was the only free time I had was when Elaine was there and she started to accuse me of being distant. She had no idea what I was doing for her. No clue. She didn't know what Siobhan was capable of and I wasn't going to tell her. In fact I wasn't going to tell her anything about Siobhan. Either my past or present with her. She didn't need that. I was enough for her to deal with.

It irked me. I was doing all this for her and I was getting nothing in return. Just shit about my lack of communication. Well, then maybe I should leave her to Siobhan. Though in truth I couldn't do that to her. If anyone deserved to be punished it was me. For what I didn't know. Some past sin I was unaware of? Either way Elaine was innocent except that she was sticking with me. That was Siobhan's gripe. She wanted me back. And the only way the malevolent cunt could think of achieving that was by getting rid of Elaine completely.

## ●●●●● Chapter Twenty Two

After a few weeks Frank rang me. Asked if I fancied meeting up for a pint. I told him I was busy. That Elaine was go through some personal difficulties and I needed to look after her. That we'd sort out something soon. Frank said "Grand" and hung up.

I wasn't going to meet him of course. Couldn't be arsed. And I had more important things to deal with.

●●●

Next time Siobhan showed up at the flat she was wearing Elaine's clothes. Elaine at her most appealing on top of that. Corset. Fishnets. Stilettoes. The clothes that had made her catch my eye in the first place. The bitch was really fucking with me now. Every other time she'd come in she'd ditched her clothes somewhere. Or most of them. And started fucking me in one way or another. What was she doing like this? It was the opposite of the sort of high priced stuff she usual wore so what the fuck was she doing in this goth stuff?

"You're really taking your time, Sean. Too much time."

"I'm not going to do it, Siobhan."

"Yes you are, Sean. Yes... you... are..."

"How the fuck do you think you're going to convince me?"

"Like this."

She pulled up her skirt and showed me the bush she'd grown out. So beautifully red that as usual it gave me an instant hard on. I dropped to my knees and started sucking on her clit.

"See, Sean, no matter what you say you're mine, you always have been."

I wanted to push her back. Tell her she was wrong. But I was captive to her cunt.

"You're my bitch, Sean."

And she looked at me in that way only she could.

"I own you. How could you ever have thought otherwise?"

I knew she was right and I knew I had to do what she said.

I had to kill Elaine.

## ●●●●● Chapter Twenty Three

We hadn't said a word to each other for over an hour. I was biding my time. I had a razor in the back pocket of my jeans and I was getting myself ready to do as Siobhan had told me to do.

"What the fuck is this, Sean?"

"What?"

"This? You and me?"

Her voice filled with anger and desperation.

"What the fuck's happened? We used to talk once."

"We still do."

"No. I talk. You nod or mumble. That's it."

"For fuck's sake, what do you want from me?"

"A relationship, Sean. That's what I want."

"All relationships get like this at times."

"No, they don't." She simply looked at me. "I've had other ones you know and none of them ever got like this."

"Maybe that's why you're not fucking in them anymore!"

"Fuck you, Sean!"

She got up from the stool she was sitting on. It was nearly time.

"I'm done with this. I'm done with pulling teeth. I'm leaving. I'll be back to get my things and you can sit in silence by yourself. You might as well be anyway."

I grabbed her. Pinned her to the wall.

"Aren't you going to say anything?"

I was screaming at her. I said it again. Silence. Then I looked at her. And it was the last time I ever would. Alive I mean. Her throat was open. My hands bloody. And there she was. Siobhan. My love. My dearest. My night. My day.

"Good boy Sean..."

I removed my clothes and then Elaine's. Siobhan entered into Elaine's lifeless body just as I did and we began to have the most sublime fuck any two creatures ever had.

●●●

"For Jesus' sake."

Frank put down his dead friend's manuscript. It had arrived in the post the same day Frank had discovered his body. Kate had rang him to ask if Frank could go round and check on Sean as she was worried about him. He'd had to kick down the door in the end before finding the lonely little twat curled up on his bed, caked in blood and smelling of his own shit. He'd called the cops and went back to the shop.

Frank threw the manuscript into a box of books he'd deemed unsellable and ready for the dump. He looked at it again.

"Fuck sake lad, if you thought killing yourself would make anyone else want to read that piece of shite you were more up your arse than I'd thought you were."

Frank locked up and went home.

## ••• THE END •••
### — *Saint Of The City* —

## THE MIGRANT by u.v. ray

"u.v.ray's novella, *The Migrant*, wasn't written to make us feel all warm and fuzzy, this is off the scale uncomfortable and from deep in the gut, the best kind of writing always is. His poetry and thoughts fly into the night, the search for human connection, he knows his place within the stars and time, believes in nothing, embracing his foibles, his anger and vision of the world."
--- Abbie Foxton, *Abbie Foxton.com*

Limited to 200 Copies
Best Novella Saboteur Award Nominee
Chapbook size / 110 pages

## DIRTY WORK by Mark SaFranko

"Whether telling us a love story that's agic and pathetically mournful (*Hating Olivia*), describing his no less glorious sexual wanderings (*Lounge Lizard*), or describing his childhood among the American losers (*God Bless America*), SaFranko always manages to turn our grimaces into broad, honest laughter."
Frederic Tue (from the introduction to *Dirty Work*)

The bridging Zajack novel between the hugely acclaimed *God Bless America* and *Hating Olivia*
Trade paperback size / 262 pages

murder slim press
since 2004
writing at the razor's edge
murderslim.com

# Murder Slim Press: Checklist

MSP#000 – *The Savage Kick #1* ft. Dan Fante ⬚
MSP#001 – *Hating Olivia* by Mark SaFranko ⬚
MSP#002 – *Role of A Lifetime* by Mark SaFranko ⬚
MSP#003 – *The Savage Kick #2* ft. Doug Stanhope ⬚
MSP#004 – *The Savage Kick #3* ft. Jim Goad ⬚
MSP#005 – *Steps* by Steve Hussy ⬚
MSP#006 – *The Angel* by Tommy Trantino ⬚
MSP#007 – *The Savage Kick #4* ft. Joe Matt ⬚
MSP#008 – *Lounge Lizard* by Mark SaFranko ⬚
MSP#009 – *Loners* by Mark SaFranko ⬚
MSP#010 – *Life Change* by Mark SaFranko ⬚
MSP#011 – *The Savage Kick #5* ft. Mark SaFranko ⬚
MSP#012 – *The Hunch* by Seymour Shubin ⬚
MSP#013 – *God Bless America* by Mark SaFranko ⬚
MSP#014 – *Lonely No More* by Seymour Shubin ⬚
MSP#015 – *The Savage Kick #6* ft. Debbie Drechsler ⬚
MSP#016 – *NAM* by Robert McGowan ⬚
MSP#017 – *A Long Perambulation* by Robert McGowan ⬚
MSP#018 – *We Are Glass* by u.v. ray ⬚
MSP#019 – *Bank Blogger* by Jeffrey P. Frye ⬚
MSP#020 – *Why Me?* by Seymour Shubin ⬚
MSP#021 – *One Crazy Day* by Jeffrey P. Frye ⬚
MSP#022 – *Spiral Out* by u.v. ray ⬚
MSP#023 – *Dirty Work* by Mark SaFranko ⬚
MSP#024 – *The Captain* by Seymour Shubin ⬚
MSP#025 – *The Savage Kick #7* ft. Carson Mell ⬚
MSP#026 – *The Migrant* by u.v. ray ⬚
MSP#027 – *Back* by Steve Hussy ⬚
MSP#028 – *Sometimes You Just...* by Mark SaFranko ⬚
MSP#029 – *The Artistic Life* by Mark SaFranko ⬚
MSP#030 – *South Main Stories* by Robert McGowan ⬚
MSP#031 – *Black Cradle* by u.v. ray ⬚
MSP#032 – *Saint Of The City* by David Noone ⬚
MSP#033 – *The Savage Kick #8* ft. Cathi Unsworth ⬚
MSP#034 – *The Savage Kick #9* ft. Mark SaFranko ⬚
MSP#035 – *Blossoms and Blood* by Mark SaFranko ⬚

murder slim press
since 2004
writing at the razor's edge
murderslim.com